W9-AUZ-191

For Justine

The polar bear lives in the Arctic. It has thick white fur to keep it warm in the Arctic winter weather. The polar bear loves nothing more than to swim in the cold, icy sea!

The giant panda lives in the mountains of China and is a protected animal. The panda loves to eat plants, especially the bamboo that grows in the forests.

Koalas live in the forests of Australia. They sleep for 20 hours each day! Years ago, koalas were thought to be bears, but now we know koalas are part of the marsupial family, along with kangaroos and wallabies.

Brown bears live in North America, Russia, and Europe. Their furry coats aren't just brown; they are sometimes yellow or black. Some brown bears grow to be 10 feet (3 m) tall when standing and can run as fast as 35 mph (56 kph)!

All sun bears love their food. They like fruit, eggs, coconuts, insects, cocoa, and honey. Sun Bears love honey so much that in their homelands of Malaysia and Indonesia, they are called "Honey Bears."

Spectacled bears live in South America. Their name comes from the beige markings on their faces around their eyes. In the rainforests, they love to climb trees, especially the tallest ones!

Written and illustrated by Barry Ablett

Designed by Gail Rose/Fernleigh Books

All rights reserved. No part of this publication may be reproduced, or stored in a retrieval system, or transmitted in any form or by any means, electronic, mechanical, photocopying, recording, or otherwise, without written permission of Tangerine Press.

Copyright © 2007 Barry Ablett

Scholastic and Tangerine Press and associated logos are trademarks of Scholastic Inc.

Published by Tangerine Press, an imprint of Scholastic Inc., 557 Broadway; New York, NY 10012

Scholastic Canada
Markham, Ontario

Scholastic Australia
Gosford, NSW

Scholastic UK
Coventry, Warwickshire

Scholastic New Zealand
Greenmount, Auckland

10 9 8 7 6 5 4 3 2 1
ISBN-10: 0-545-00068-8
ISBN-13: 978-0-545-00068-0
Made in China

Dear
Polar Bear...

Barry Ablett

tangerine press

an imprint of
SCHOLASTIC
www.scholastic.com

Polar Bear was unhappy.

His igloo was so empty and cold. Brrr!

Polar Bear thought about his friend, Koala, who lived in a forest full of trees and flowers. Maybe he could send something to brighten up Polar Bear's home. So Polar Bear sat down to write a letter.

Postman Penguin came to collect it.

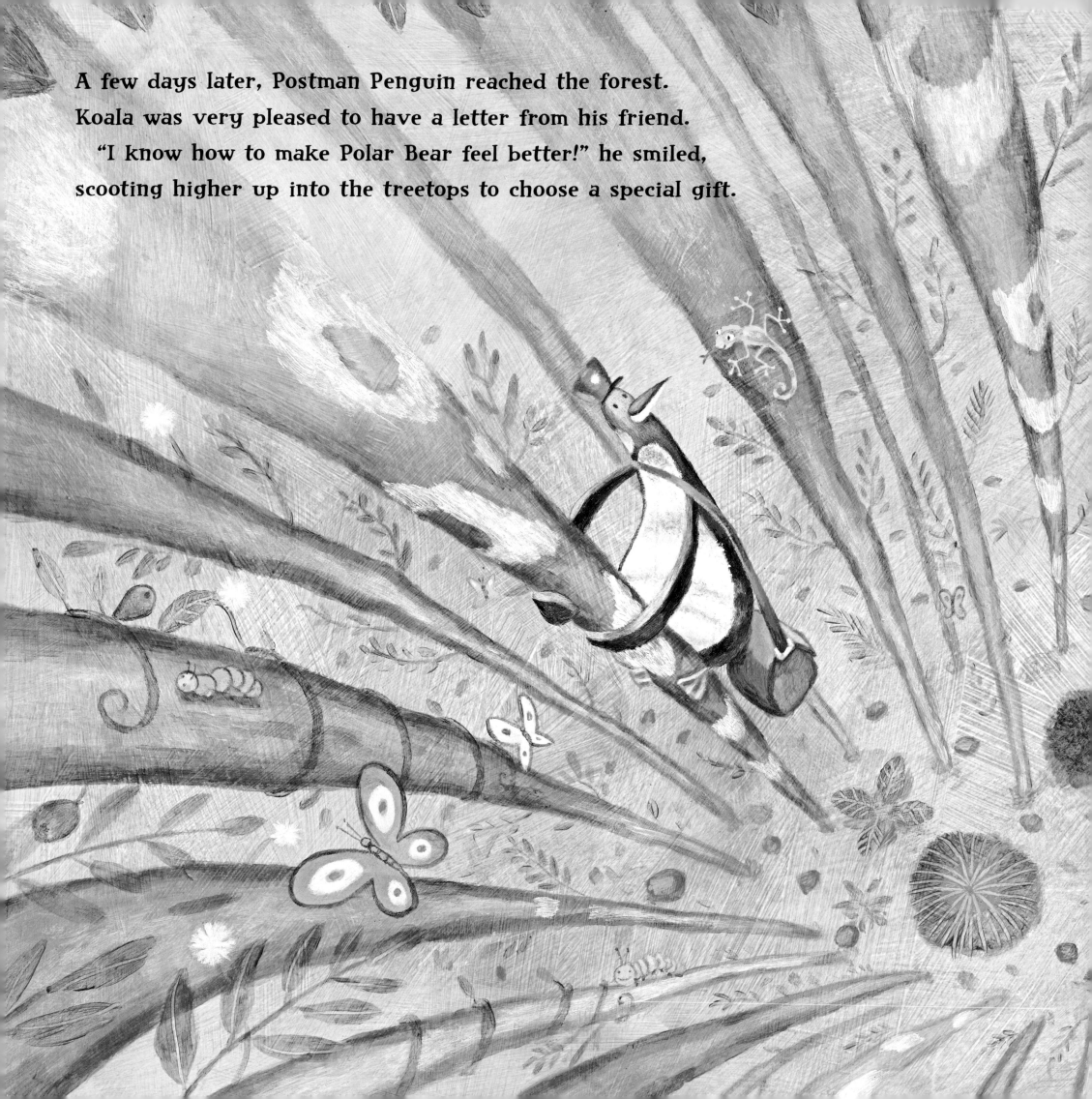

A few days later, Postman Penguin reached the forest.
Koala was very pleased to have a letter from his friend.
   "I know how to make Polar Bear feel better!" he smiled,
scooting higher up into the treetops to choose a special gift.

Polar Bear opened Koala's package as soon as it arrived.

  "How exciting!" he giggled, as he read the letter inside.
Then he planted the seeds and made a nice home for the caterpillars.

Polar Bear's tummy rumbled. He wanted something yummy to eat,
but all his food was icy and cold.

"I know," Polar Bear thought. "I'll write to Sun Bear in the rainforest. Maybe he can send me something tasty to eat."
And he sat down to write another letter.

Sun Bear was busy eating some delicious honey
when Postman Penguin arrived.

"Cold, icy food? Poor Polar Bear!" Sun Bear slurped.
"I'll send him a special sweet treat."

To Sun Bear
Coconut Forest
Malaysia

The next morning, Polar Bear had a surprise from Sun Bear.

"Soft, sticky honey—yum, yum!" he hummed. "And, best of all, it's not frozen!"

Polar Bear's tummy was full now, but he wished his igloo was a little warmer.

"I wonder how Panda keeps warm," Polar Bear said to himself.

And he sat down to write another letter.

To Panda
Bamboo Glade
The Great Forest
China

When Postman Penguin arrived, Panda was taking a nap.
"A letter from Polar Bear?" Panda yawned. "And he wants
something to keep him warm? I've got just what he needs!"

"Thank you, Panda!" Polar Bear laughed as he opened his
present. But then he frowned, looking at the strange creatures.
"How will these keep me warm? Oh, what am I to do?"
he sighed, feeling lonely. "I wish my friends
weren't so far away."

Then Polar Bear thought of Brown Bear. "She always
knows just what to do!" And he sat down
to write another letter.

The next day, Postman Penguin found Brown Bear and her cubs playing by the river.

"Oh dear," said Brown Bear as she read the letter. "Polar Bear sounds very lonely. I think he needs a pet to cheer him up!"

A few days later, Polar Bear opened the package from Brown Bear and looked inside. He stared at the fish, and the fish stared back.

"I'll call you Bubbles," Polar Bear smiled.

To Polar Bear
Icicle Igloo
North Pole
The Arctic

"And I'll get you some fresh water for your bowl."

But it was very dark outside.

"I wish I could see a bit better," Polar Bear squinted. "My friend
Spectacled Bear can see in the dark—maybe he can help me.
Wait, Postman Penguin! I've got one more letter for you!"

To Spectacled Bear
Amazon Rainforest
Peru

Spectacled Bear was finishing his dinner when
he saw Postman Penguin climbing over the rocks.
"A letter from Polar Bear!" smiled Spectacled Bear. "He can't
see in the dark, eh? I have the perfect present for him."

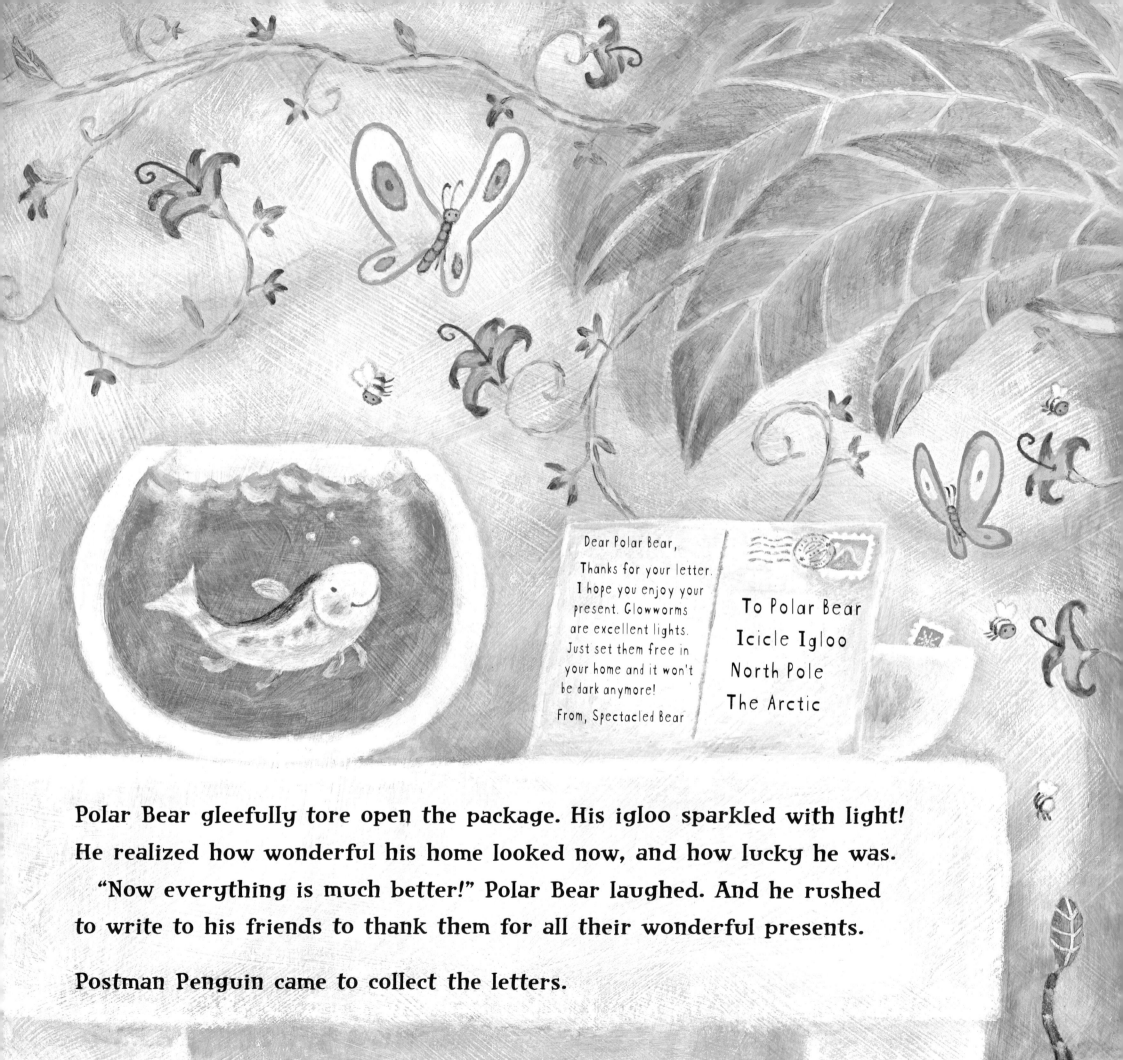

Dear Polar Bear,

Thanks for your letter.
I hope you enjoy your
present. Glowworms
are excellent lights.
Just set them free in
your home and it won't
be dark anymore!

From, Spectacled Bear

To Polar Bear
Icicle Igloo
North Pole
The Arctic

Polar Bear gleefully tore open the package. His igloo sparkled with light! He realized how wonderful his home looked now, and how lucky he was.

"Now everything is much better!" Polar Bear laughed. And he rushed to write to his friends to thank them for all their wonderful presents.

Postman Penguin came to collect the letters.

Polar Bear waited and waited, but no letters came back.

"I think my friends have forgotten about me, Bubbles," he sniffed.

Then, suddenly, there was a KNOCK-KNOCK at the door....

"Is that for me?" Polar Bear gasped. "What on Earth could be inside it?" He ran over and opened the box....